Printed in the U.S.A.

ISBN 0-7172-8270-8

Flip Flap Flop

A Book About Self-Esteem

By Stephanie St. Pierre • Illustrated by Joe Ewers

GROLIER

"What a terrific day," said Kermit. He and Fozzie and Gonzo had been fishing in the creek. "Yeah," Fozzie agreed. "It's too bad we have to go now."

"And I was just finding some really neat junk for my collection," said Gonzo. He held up the end of his fishing rod to show his friends what he had caught.

"That's weird!" said Fozzie. Kermit made a face. Gonzo carefully took the junk off his fishing hook and stuffed it into his knapsack.

"That's why I like it!" he said with a laugh. "Weird is my middle name!"

"We'd better get going, guys," said Kermit. "My mom won't be happy if I'm late for dinner."

"I know a shortcut," Gonzo suggested. "You go under the bridge and then up over the hill."

So Kermit, Fozzie, and Gonzo headed for the bridge.

Flip, flap, flop.   Flip, flap, flop.   Flip, flap, flop.
"Hey, what's that?" asked Gonzo. His voice echoed under the small bridge. They all stopped. The funny flip-flap-flopping sound stopped, too.
"Come on," Kermit said. "Let's get out of here." It was pretty dark under the bridge. And the echo made it seem kind of spooky.

Kermit ran ahead of Gonzo and Fozzie. *Flip, flap, flop. Flip, flap, flop.* There it was again. The sound echoed loudly.

Kermit was a little scared. Then he heard Fozzie and Gonzo laughing.

"It's just your wet feet!" Gonzo said.

"It's his wet, *floppy* feet!" Fozzie added.

Kermit stopped and looked at his friends. Then he looked down at his feet.

"It's not me," mumbled Kermit. He felt very embarrassed.

He started to walk away, but as he did, the sound followed him. *Flip, flap, flop.* It was quieter now that he was out from under the bridge, but he still could hear it. He'd never noticed how funny his feet could sound. Now every step he took made him feel uncomfortable.

Fozzie and Gonzo followed Kermit, trying to slap their feet down on the road to make the same funny noise.

"Talk about weird," Gonzo said. "That's the weirdest sound I've ever heard."

"I think Kermit has the weirdest feet ever," said Fozzie.

Gonzo and Fozzie laughed and talked all the way home. Neither of them noticed that Kermit didn't laugh at all. In fact, he was very quiet.

When he got home, Kermit didn't even say good-bye to his friends. He went straight inside.

"What's wrong with him?" wondered Fozzie.

"Maybe he's worried about being late," said Gonzo.

"That means we're late, too!" cried Fozzie. So Fozzie and Gonzo said good-bye to each other and raced to their own homes.

At bedtime, Kermit couldn't fall asleep. He sat up in bed and stared at his feet. He wondered if *all* his friends thought his feet were funny. Maybe everyone had been laughing at him all along!

And what if it weren't just his feet they were laughing at? Maybe it was his wide, green face. Or his long, skinny arms. Or maybe it was his voice or the way he dressed.

By the time Kermit fell asleep, he was sure that everything about himself must be wrong.

The next day, Kermit didn't want to get up.

"I don't feel well," he told his mother. But she could see that he wasn't sick.

Finally he left for school. He knew everyone would be waiting at the corner. *By now,* he thought miserably, *Fozzie and Gonzo have probably told everybody about my feet.*

Sure enough, the other kids were laughing when Kermit met up with them...but as soon as they saw him, they stopped. Kermit felt terrible. He dragged his feet. He stared at the sidewalk. He didn't want to talk to anyone. And when he saw Gonzo and Fozzie whispering, he felt even worse. He was sure they were talking about him.

All day long, Kermit worried. At lunchtime, he wanted to sit with Piggy and Gonzo. But what if they didn't *really* want to sit with him?

As Kermit walked over to them, he heard Piggy talking. "I don't know what's wrong with him," she was saying. Then Gonzo saw Kermit and told Piggy to be quiet. But it was too late. Kermit hurried away.

"Wait, Kermie," called Piggy.

"Come back!" called Gonzo.

After school, the kids had softball practice. Mr. Bumper was coaching the team. Kermit usually loved softball, but not today. When it was his turn at bat, he got a hit. But he didn't want to run. He was tagged out at first base and dragged his feet all the way back to the bench.

"That was a good hit, Kermit," said Mr. Bumper. "But you didn't even try to get on base."

"I can't run anymore," Kermit said sadly.

"Why not?" asked Mr. Bumper.

"I just can't," Kermit said. He was embarrassed to tell Mr. Bumper the real reason. He was afraid his feet would flap and that his friends would laugh at him.

"You know," Mr. Bumper said after a moment, "it might help to talk about it."

Kermit stared at his feet. Then he looked up at Mr. Bumper.

"It's all because of my stupid feet," he blurted out.

Then he told Mr. Bumper how bad he felt. He told him how worried he was about everything and how afraid he was that his friends didn't really like him.

"But, Kermit," said Mr. Bumper, "that isn't true. You have lots of friends who like you. And the things you're worried about are the very things that make you special. They make you *you*!

"Your feet may be kind of flat," Mr. Bumper went on, "and make a funny noise when they're wet. But that's not bad...it's just *different*. Piggy and Fozzie and Gonzo are all different in their own ways, too."

Kermit thought about that for a moment.

"If those guys really are my friends," he finally asked, "then why did they laugh at me? And whisper about me? And talk about me behind my back?"

Just then, Fozzie and Gonzo raced over. "Why don't you ask them?" said Mr. Bumper.

"What's the matter with Kermit?" Fozzie asked.

"Are you sick or something?" said Gonzo.

"I'm okay," Kermit said. "I was upset because you laughed at me, and I heard you talking to Piggy about me, and..."

"But we were talking about how worried we are about you," said Gonzo.

"You've been acting so weird," said Fozzie.

Kermit frowned. "It's my feet that are weird," he muttered.

That's when Gonzo and Fozzie remembered laughing at Kermit's funny feet. Suddenly they understood.

"We didn't mean to make you sad," said Fozzie. "We're sorry we laughed at you."

"You're our friend," said Gonzo. "We like you *and* your feet."

When Kermit thought about *that*, he felt a whole lot better.

"Let's get back to the game," he said. "I've got to make up for the out I made before!"

Kermit, Fozzie, and Gonzo hurried onto the field. As Kermit ran, he thought he could hear his feet going *flip, flap, flop*. But this time, the only one who laughed was Kermit.

Let's Talk About Self-Esteem

Is there anything you don't like about yourself? Something that makes you feel funny?

For a while, Kermit's feet made him feel funny. But he learned that they're two of the things that make him special!

Here are some questions about self-esteem for you to think about:

What are some of the things that make *you* special?

Have you ever been teased about anything? How did you feel about it?

Do you think there's some way you could have stopped it?